D1622866

Konnichiwa!

I Am a
Japanese-American Girl

Tricia Brown

Photographs by
Kazuyoshi Arai

Henry Holt and Company
New York

Henry Holt and Company, Inc.
Publishers since 1866
115 West 18th Street
New York, New York 10011

Henry Holt is a registered
trademark of Henry Holt and Company, Inc.

Text copyright © 1995 by Tricia Brown
Photographs copyright © 1995 by Kazuyoshi Arai
All rights reserved.
Published in Canada by Fitzhenry & Whiteside Ltd.,
195 Allstate Parkway, Markham, Ontario L3R 4T8.

Library of Congress Cataloging-in-Publication Data
Brown, Tricia.
Konnichiwa! I am a Japanese-American girl / Tricia Brown;
photographs by Kazuyoshi Arai.
p.   cm.
1. Kamiya, Lauren Seiko—Juvenile literature.   2. Japanese
Americans—California—San Francisco—Social life and customs—
Juvenile literature.   3. Japanese Americans—Social life and
customs—Juvenile literature.   4. San Francisco (Calif.)—Social
life and customs—Juvenile literature.   I. Arai, Kazuyoshi.
II. Title.   III. Title: I am a Japanese-American girl.
F869.S39J33   1995   973'.04956—dc20   94-36107

ISBN 0-8050-2353-4

First Edition—1995

Printed in the United States of America
on acid-free paper. ∞

10 9 8 7 6 5 4 3 2 1

Acknowledgments

The author and photographer gratefully acknowledge the following persons without whose support, enthusiasm, and cooperation this book would not have been possible: the Kamiya family—Stanley, Alice, Lauren, and Sherry; Mrs. Masano Kamiya; Madame Rokushige Fujima; V. Kanani Choy, principal, Clarendon School; Sharon Chang, secretary, Clarendon School; the Takatani family—Tetsu, Grace, Shohei, and Kohei; the teachers, parents, and students of Clarendon School; Christine Hiroshima, Day of Remembrance Curriculum Committee; Sego Oka and Paul Osaki, Japanese-American historians; Kimochi Senior Center; the Japanese Cultural and Community Center of Northern California; National Japanese Historical Society; Japanese-American Citizens League; Seiichi Tanaka; San Francisco Taiko Dojo; Katsura Garden; Ikenobo Ikebana Society; Kinokuniya Book Stores of America; Klara M. Ma, chairperson, Cherry Blossom Festival; Dr. Anita DeFrantz, University of San Francisco; Mr. and Mrs. Ginji Mizutani; Dr. and Mrs. George Goodman; Ms. Amy Goodman; Kathy Fukami Ginsburg; John Philbrook and Linda Gerstlinger, children's librarians; San Francisco Public Library; Cheryl Schoffstoll; Elizabeth G. Tufts; Thomas N. Tufts; Tani Edwards; Barrett Brown; Andrea Brown; and our editor, Simone Kaplan.

For Yoko,
my childhood friend,
and her family,
who welcomed me
into their
Japanese-American
home; and of course,
to the Kamiya
family, especially
Lauren Seiko
and Sherry Noriko…
domo arigato…
—T. B.

Konnichiwa! My name is Lauren Seiko Kamiya. I am a Japanese-American girl.

Here I am with my younger sister, Sherry Noriko. We are dressed in *kimono*s—the clothing that's traditionally worn by Japanese people.

We are so excited. This weekend we will celebrate the Cherry Blossom Festival!

Spring is a special time in Japan, a country where everyone appreciates
the beauty of nature. At the beginning of spring, my sister and I welcome
the season by dancing at the Japanese Tea Garden in Golden Gate Park.
In Japan viewing the cherry blossoms is a family event.

In San Francisco where I live, the cherry blossom season has become a time to honor and celebrate Japanese-American culture. For two weekends in April, Japanese-Americans from all over Northern California come together to take part in the Cherry Blossom Festival in San Francisco's Japantown.

Even the kids at my school prepare for the event weeks ahead. Here is a photo of my school, Clarendon. It is a public school. As you can see, it is like any American school. The only difference is we learn Japanese as well as English. Anyone who is interested in learning Japanese language and culture can go to our school.

"FAN"TASTIC !

ひなまつり

In spring, it's hard to keep our minds on schoolwork! Many of us learn Japanese traditional arts, and we present our skills at the Cherry Blossom Festival. We will be marching in the parade and some of us will be doing special things.

These kids are practicing their *taiko* drums for the parade. The real drums are made out of wood and hide. They make a very powerful sound. These rubber tires are used only for rehearsal as the real drums are too loud to practice on!

Here is my friend, Seiji, practicing his *shakuhachi*. This bamboo flute looks simple to play, but actually the instrument is difficult to master. Seiji will be giving a concert on his flute.

Sherry and I are classical dancers. We will be rehearsing for our festival performance at our dance teacher's house later this week.

Since both of my parents work until late every day, our grandmothers take turns watching us after school.

Today my father's mother, Grandma Kamiya, is taking care of us.

Grandma is *nisei,* which means the second generation of American immigrants. Her parents came to America from Japan, and she was born and raised here. During World War II, the United States was at war with Japan and some people were worried about whether Japanese-Americans were loyal to America or Japan. Japanese-Americans were sent away to camps, where they had to stay until the war was over. Grandma tells us about that time. It was terrible for all the Japanese-Americans. But fortunately for her, something good came out of it: she met my grandfather there!

Now the American government has apologized for what happened to their Japanese-American citizens, and February 19 has been named the Day of Remembrance. This is the day when we remember what happened way back then.

Today Grandma Kamiya is taking us to Japantown, the shopping center in San Francisco where stores sell Japanese things and all the restaurants serve Japanese food. This is where the Cherry Blossom Festival will take place. A tourist stops and asks for directions. We show her the way.

Before we begin shopping, we want to have lunch. *Ooooh,* there are so many good things to choose from!

There is *sushi,* which is raw fish on top of vinegared rice; *sashimi,* which is raw fish… I like tempura *donburi*—rice with deep-fried shrimp and vegetables on top. Japanese food is delicious, but don't get me wrong: I like hamburgers, too!

When we're eating Japanese food, we use chopsticks. They are called *o-hashi.* It's fun! My grandmother likes noodles for lunch. You know what? In Japan, it's acceptable to make slurping noises when you eat noodles!

After lunch, we like to spend the whole afternoon at the Japantown mall. The bookstore is my grandmother's favorite, so it's our first stop. Japanese books are generally different from American books. Most are read from right to left and the words are read from top to bottom!

My sister likes the *bonsai* store. Bonsai is the Japanese art form of raising miniature trees and plants. The gardeners work very hard. They prune the roots once a year and take care of the trees to keep them very small. The branches and twigs are trimmed and are often wired. It is not how small the bonsai are that is important; what matters is how well they represent the beauty and majesty of nature.

My favorite is the *futon* store. A futon is a special kind of mattress that most Japanese people sleep on. In Japan, people put their futons on straw mats called *tatami* that cover the floor. Here in America, people place their futons on the floor or on frames. Futons come in many pretty colors and designs.

Sherry and I both admire the flower arrangements at the Ikebana Society. *Ikebana* is a kind of flower arranging. There are only a few flowers used in the arrangement and everything has symbolic meaning, even the vase!

At the end of the day, we pay a visit to the Japanese Cultural and Community Center where my grandmother wants to check her volunteer work schedule. She will serve lunches to senior citizens there tomorrow. The community center has many activities for all age groups. Here is one of my grandmother's friends practicing a song with the *karaoke* for a program that will take place later on today. The karaoke plays recorded music and you can sing along with it.

It has been a fun day but now it is time to go home. We always enjoy going to Japantown with our grandmother.

Every other day my mother's mother takes care of us. She was born in Japan, and we call her *O-baachan,* which means grandmother in Japanese. Although O-baachan has been here for many years, she still keeps most of her Japanese traditions. Her name is Madame Rokushige Fujima, and she has a famous Japanese classical dance school in San Francisco. The mayor of San Francisco even named a day in her honor! Here she is showing Sherry and me the plaque he gave her for her cultural contribution to the community.

O-baachan knows many of the traditional Japanese arts, and she looks forward to Sherry and my visits so she can share them with us. Surprise! She is our classical dance teacher! Later on today, we are going to practice the dances we will perform for the Cherry Blossom Festival.

O-baachan is also a gifted painter. Classical Japanese art is inspired by nature. Here you can see her watercolor paintings of flowers and plants. The picture in the back is of Mount Fuji, the most famous mountain in Japan.

In this photograph, O-baachan is contrasting one of her small paintings with the big one my grandfather painted. As you can see, being artistic runs in the family!

She teaches us calligraphy, too. It is called *shodo*. The idea is to make the characters very beautiful. We use a special brush. Here we are writing our names...oops! I spilled some ink!

Sometimes, my sister and I do *origami*. This is the Japanese art of paper folding. I can make all kinds of animals, birds, and flowers out of a simple piece of paper. Here I am teaching Sherry how to make the crane, a symbol of long life.

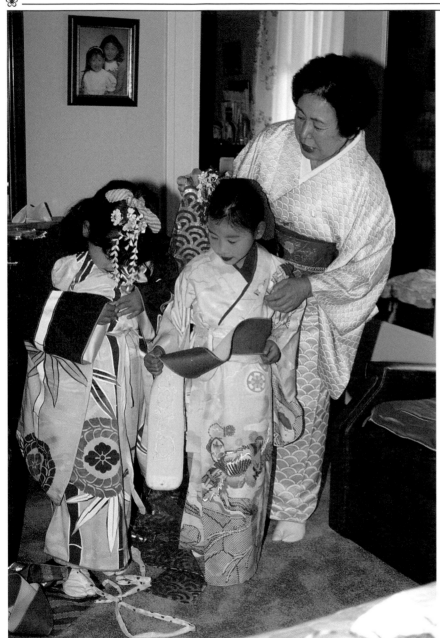

Now it is time to rehearse the dances that we'll perform at the festival. First, O-baachan helps us put on our kimonos. They are made of silk and as you can see, they come in many beautiful colors. The sash is very wide and called the *obi*. It is tied in a very special way.

We go outside to take photographs. When we come back, we take off our shoes. It is the Japanese custom to take off your shoes at the door and not to wear shoes indoors.

Another custom is to bow slightly as a sign of respect to another person.
On formal occasions, the lower one bows, the more respect one shows.
Before we begin our dance class, we always bow to our grandmother,
our teacher.

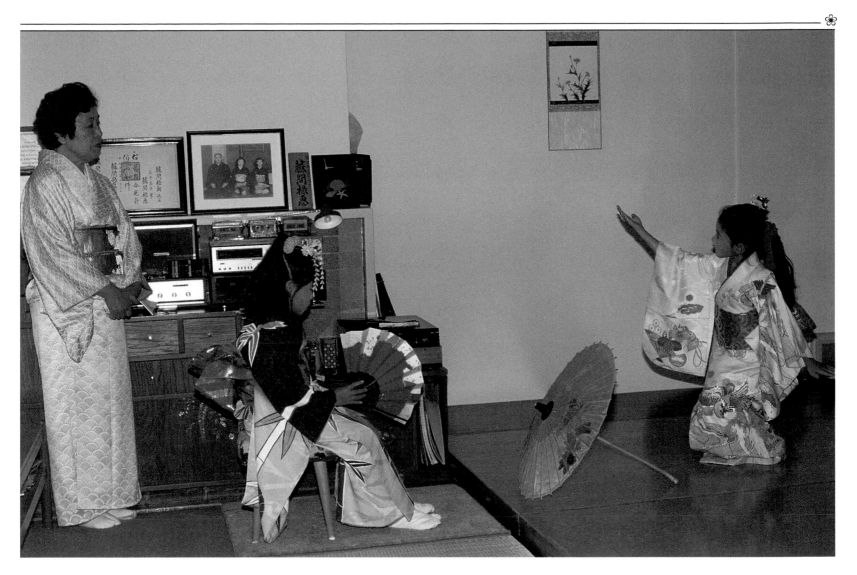

For the Cherry Blossom Festival, Sherry will be dancing a happy dance...

…but mine is sad. It tells a traditional story that's four hundred years old.

When we finish our rehearsal, we have tea. Japanese tea is called *O-cha*. It's called green tea in English because it's made with green leaves and tastes different from black tea. We talk with our grandmother about our rehearsal. She is pleased with our progress and thinks we are ready to dance at the festival recital, which is only two days away!

It's finally here! The first weekend of the Cherry Blossom Festival. Sherry and I hurriedly get dressed and eat breakfast.

We've got to help our mom pack the car.

We're going to help O-baachan and her students sell *gyoza*. These are dumplings filled with minced pork and vegetable, and they're delicious. We sell gyoza to raise money for O-baachan's dance school. More than thirty stalls in the festival's food bazaar sell samples of typical Japanese foods to raise money for nonprofit community groups.

I spend most of the day in the trailer behind the stall putting the minced pork and vegetable filling in the gyoza. It's a lot of work!

Look around the festival.
There are games to play
such as fishing, bingo, and darts....

…And there are things to buy, such as these T-shirts that help support my school! And many, many things to see…

This man is a cartoonist,

and here are the students from the *taiko dojo* getting ready to perform on their drums.

I like to watch Seiji's father pounding steamed rice into rice cakes. These are called *mochi*. This event is traditionally performed at New Year's, but here at the festival they want to show everyone how it is done.

This little girl is playing her *koto*, a classical Japanese instrument.

And here are some boys demonstrating *karate,* which is a martial art.

These girls are all vying for the title of Queen of the Cherry Blossom Festival.

Dance performances take place all day.
People of all ages dance.

Here is my mother dancing on
the stage. Isn't she lovely?
She takes a special bow
during the finale.

On the last day of the festival is the Japanese-style grand parade. There will be taiko drummers, colorful costumes, and the shrine called the *mikoshi*. This shrine traditionally appears at the end of the parade. It is filled with fruits, flowers, foodstuffs, and *sake*—Japanese rice wine—as offerings to the gods. The more it is rocked up and down throughout the parade, the more good blessings will be sent to the people watching it.

And guess who else is in the parade? You're right…me!

While my mother, Sherry, and I get ready, my dad decorates the truck he will drive. It'll carry the speakers that broadcast the music we need for our dance school.

All of us dance down the street during the parade—

even my grandmother!

And to you, now that the parade is over and this story has come to its end, I'll say, *sayonara*. That means "good-bye" in Japanese. I hope you enjoyed meeting me and learning about my life as a Japanese-American girl.

Glossary

Bonsai (BON-sigh): Japanese art form of cultivating miniature trees.

Donburi (DON-bury): Rice topped with meat, fish, and/or vegetables.

Dojo (doe-joe): Exercise hall, gymnasium.

Futon (foo-ton): Mattress that most Japanese people sleep on.

Gyoza (gio-za): Dumpling with wonton wrapping and pork and vegetable filling.

Ikebana (EE-KEH-ba-na): Japanese flower arranging.

Karaoke (ka-ra-o-keh): Recorded musical backing for vocal accompaniment.

Karate (ka-RA-teh): A martial art that emphasizes discipline and technique.

Kimono (kee-mo-no): Traditional Japanese dress.

Konnichiwa (kon-nee-chee-wa): "Hello" in Japanese.

Mikoshi (me-co-shi): Shrine carried during festivals.

Mochi (mo-chee): Rice cake; traditionally eaten on New Year's Day.

Nisei (KNEE-see): Second generation of American immigrants.

O-baachan (O-BAA-chan): Japanese for grandmother.

O-cha (o-cha): Japanese tea; known as "green tea," because it is made with green leaves.

Obi (oh-bee): Japanese belt or sash worn with a kimono.

O-hashi (o-hash-ee): A pair of chopsticks.

Origami (O-REE-ga-mi): Japanese paper folding.

Sake (sa-keeh): Rice wine.

Sashimi (sa-she-me): Raw fish.

Sayonara (sa-yo-na-ra): "Good-bye" in Japanese.

Shakuhachi (sha-koo-ha-chi): Bamboo flute.

Shodo (SHOW-doe): Japanese calligraphy.

Sushi (sue-she): Raw fish on vinegared rice.

Taiko (tie-ko): Japanese drums made out of wood and hide.

Tatami (ta-tam-ee): A woven straw mat.

Reading List

Coerr, Eleanor. *Sadako and the Thousand Cranes*. New York: Putnam, 1977.

Davis, Daniel S. *Behind Barbed Wire: The Imprisonment of Japanese Americans During World War II*. New York: Dutton, 1982.

Downer, Lesley. *Japanese Food and Drink*. New York: Bookwright Press, 1988.

Elkin, Judith. *A Family in Japan*. Photographs by Stuart Atkin. Chicago: Lerner Publications, Co., 1987.

Friedman, Ina R. *How My Parents Learned to Eat*. Boston: Houghton Mifflin, 1984.

Hamanaka, Sheila. *The Journey: Japanese Americans, Racism and Renewal*. New York: Orchard Books, 1990.

Hondo, Isae. *How to Make Origami: The Art of Japanese Paper Folding*. New York: McDowell, Obolensky, 1959.

Hongo, Florence, general editor. *Japanese American Journey: The Story of a People*. San Mateo: Japanese Curriculum Project, 1985.

Hoobler, Dorothy and Thomas Hoobler. *Aloha Means Come Back: The Story of a World War II Girl*. Silver Burdett Press, 1992.

Kitano, Harry. *The Japanese Americans*. New York: Chelsea House, 1988.

Means, Florence C. *The Moved-Outers*. New York: Walker and Co., 1993.

Savin, Marcia. *The Moon Bridge*. New York: Scholastic, 1992.

Say, Allen. *Feast of Lanterns*. New York: Harper and Row, 1976.

——. *Grandfather's Journey*. New York: Houghton Mifflin, 1993.

——. *Once Under the Cherry Blossom Tree: An Old Japanese Tale*. New York: Harper and Row, 1974.

——. *The Inn-Keeper's Apprentice*. New York, 1976.

——. *Tree of Cranes*. New York: Houghton Mifflin, 1991.

Shigekawa, Marlene. *Bluejay in the Desert*. Polychrome Publishers, 1993.

Snyder, Dianne. *The Boy of the Three-Year Nap*. Houghton Mifflin, 1988.

Soto, Gary. *Pacific Crossing*. New York: Harcourt Brace, 1992.

Takashima, Shizuye. *A Child in Prison Camp*. Plattsburgh, N.Y.: Tundra Books, 1989.

Uchida, Yoshiko. *A Jar of Dreams*. New York: Macmillan, 1981.

Uchida, Yoshiko. *Best Bad Thing*. New York: Macmillan, 1983.